Heartsong

For Rose and Grace – K.C-H

For Wicky and John Hawkins – J.R

Based on the true life of
Antonio Lucio Vivaldi
4th March 1678 – 28th July 1741

ORCHARD BOOKS
Carmelite House
50 Victoria Embankment
London EC4Y 0DZ
First published in 2015 by Orchard Books
This edition published in 2016 by The Watts Publishing Group
ISBN 978 1 40833 607 6
Text © Kevin Crossley-Holland 2015
Illustrations © Jane Ray 2015
The rights of Kevin Crossley-Holland to be identified as the author and of Jane
Ray to be identified as the illustrator of this work have been asserted by them in
accordance with the Copyright, Designs and Patents Act, 1988.
A CIP catalogue record for this book is available from the British Library.
2 4 6 8 10 9 7 5 3 1
Printed in China
Orchard Books
An imprint of Hachette Children's Group
Part of The Watts Publishing Group Limited
An Hachette UK Company
www.hachette.co.uk

MIX
Paper from
responsible sources
FSC
www.fsc.org
FSC® C104740

Heartsong

A short novel by
Kevin Crossley-Holland

Illustrated by Jane Ray

ORCHARD

Plink …

plink …

PLASH …

plink …

There's a little pool of rainwater in one corner of my room.

Sometimes the drops of water falling from the ceiling onto the stone floor sound like musical notes.

They sound like a song I almost think I almost know.

I can't remember the first day I came here. Of course I can't. Sometimes I dream I can, but I can't.

It was a day in early autumn, more than eight years ago. I didn't come through the door. And I didn't come in through a window, or down the chimney.

Mother Paulina says I came in the normal way: I was pushed through the baby hatch.

*

Almost all the girls and boys here came when they were babies. Some were only two or three days old. But Mother Paulina says I was a very late arrival. She and the other nuns think I was already six months old.

Just before daybreak, or just after dusk, or else in the quiet time during the middle of a hot day, a young mother steals up to the wooden door of the orphanage. She is trembling. Her heart is hammering and her breath is jerky. Then she delivers her baby through the hatch.

The young mother knocks at the door as a sign that there's a new arrival and, sobbing and shaking, she runs away.

*

This is the home of unwanted children. Most of us are brought here, a few are found, and almost all of us come wearing rags, or naked as needles. Almost none come with a name.

*

I've seen what happens.

The porter carries the baby into a bare stone room and lays her – it's usually a girl – at one end of a big table. Then Sister Oliva examines her in case she has sores or scabs, or lice in her hair. A second sister, she's called Cattina, sits down at the other end of the table and carefully writes the time and date, and what clothes the new baby is wearing, and

whether her mother has left any kind of gift.
Her black writing is as spindly as a spider's legs.

What happens next is horrible.

Sister Cattina stands up and thrusts a metal
rod with a square end into the burning fire,
and she only takes it out when it's pulsing and
red-hot. She presses the end of the rod against
the baby's left arm. Just below her shoulder.
The baby screams and screams. And when her
wound heals, you can see the letter P with
a cross below it stamped on her arm.

'It's for your own good,' Sister Cattina told
me. 'What would you do if someone stole you,
and made you work for him? The stamp is so
you can always prove you belong here.'

*

Sometimes a mother leaves a little gift to help
the nuns pay for her baby's clothing, and
some mothers leave a token so that they can
recognise their children if ever they're able
to come back and claim them.

My friends used to talk about
what they brought with them.
Angelica says her mother left a glass
necklace and Anna says a bronze

crucifix and Julia says a silver coin.
Peta's mother left half a token, a
bronze medal of Saint Mark, tucked

into her swaddling clothes.

'What about you, Laura?' they
asked. 'Didn't your mother leave
anything? Nothing at all?'

'Maybe Laura's mother hadn't
anything to give,' Mother Paulina
interrupted them. 'Maybe she was a
beggar, and she's not the only one.

At least she brought Laura here.'

Several girls lowered their eyes.
I know that Rosana was found in
a gloomy passage, and Aneta was

floating in a basket along a canal.
The nuns fished her out.

*

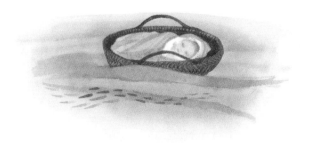

I can't remember my mother and I don't
know why she had to leave me here. But if
ever I saw her again – and if only I could
speak – I'd say: I've thought about you every
day. Have you thought about me? I'd say: The
nuns gave me the name of Laura, and I often
think that's my true name, too.

I'd ask: Who is my father? Do I have sisters
or brothers? Have I been mute since the day
I was born, or could I squeak or sob or gurgle?
Do you love music too?

*

After my mother left me here, I was soon sent

away again. Almost at once, in fact. That's what happens to all the babies here.

They're carried away to safe homes in the countryside. Wet nurses suckle them, knit clothes for them, and teach them to talk. They don't come back to the orphanage until they're six or seven.

My home was a wooden hut with a roof like a hat that was much too big for it.

That was where Berto the butcher and his wife, Eva, lived.

'I really don't know about you, Laura,' said Eva, my wet nurse. 'You've got a throat; you've got a tongue. So why can't you speak?'

I crooked my arms and showed her the palms of my hands. I shook my head.

'Though mind you,' she went on, 'I did hear of a boy who lived in the next valley, years ago that was, and he never said a single word until his fifth birthday. On that very morning, as soon as he woke up, he sang out: "I'm five! I'm five! Saints alive! It's time I got myself a wife!"'

Eva snorted with laughter.

But it's true. I've got a throat. I've got a tongue. Why can't I speak?

I wish I could.

*

When I was six and still living with Eva and Berto, I fell ill. To begin with, Eva thought I was just being lazy when I signed that I felt too tired and weak to go up to the high pasture with our cows.

'You're not a mouse or a rabbit,' she said. 'You're as spirited as a foal. Now get on with

it!' And she cuffed me round both ears.

For most of the time, I just lay on my straw bed, worn out, and sometimes I could hear Berto and Eva telling their friends:

'A reckling, that's what she is.'

'Something inside her is eating away at her. First her voice, now this. Come Christmas, she'll be deep in the earth.'

I wasn't though. I wasn't. And the slow seasons passed...

I can't say why I began to recover, any more than I can say why I fell ill. I started to eat, my body grew stronger, I stood up, and reached out for the sun.

'If God has spared you,' Eva told me, 'it must be for some purpose.'

So I didn't come back to Venice until I was eight.

I rode behind Eva, and Berto rode beside us.

As we trotted down to the banks of the lagoon, the autumn sun was setting. Its blood spilled and stained the water. Then all the towers and churches began to glow and the church bells called out to us.

'The island of Venice,' the butcher told me, 'is the largest city in the world.'

'And the most beautiful,' Eva added.

By the time we had stabled the two horses, the sun had set. A boatman rowed us over to

the city, and from there we walked along a path beside a wide canal. There were grand houses on either side of us. Then another canal crossed ours, and we had to climb over a bridge. It was very steep.

'Most of the streets in Venice are made of water,' the butcher's wife told me. 'This city is like your own body, criss-crossed with veins and arteries.'

I walked between them towards the orphanage. It towered over me and looked very grim.

*

Mother Paulina greets each of us on the day
we return. 'Welcome home!' she says, and she
stoops and embraces us.

But the orphanage didn't feel like home.
It didn't wrap around my shoulders like Berto
and Eva's wooden hut.

'Welcome, Little Sister!' That's what the
girls say.

'Welcome to the prison!' say the boys.

*

To begin with, I was given a bed in the
dormitory for new girls with the other girls
who had just come back from their foster-
parents and safe homes in the country. There
were thirteen of us.

I'd only met a few girls of my age before,
and I'd never been surrounded by so many
people except when Berto and Eva took me
with them to the fair. I felt very shy.

Anyhow, I couldn't speak.

At night, I lay and listened as the girls

whispered and giggled. Now and then I tried to sign to them, and to begin with they were interested and copied me, but it wasn't long before they grew impatient.

A few days after I came back from the butcher's family, Sister Cattina led me to the music room where Father Antonio was waiting for me, sitting at his harpsichord. He's our music-master, and he tests each girl here.

Father Antonio has flaming red hair. I've heard some of the older girls say he's the most handsome man in Venice, and the greatest composer there has ever been, and that if he wasn't a priest they would marry him.

'This is Laura,' Sister Cattina said. 'She can't sing.'

'That's for me to decide,' replied Father Antonio.

'I mean, she hasn't got a voice.'

'Ahh!' exclaimed Father Antonio. He nodded, and then he gave me a gentle smile. 'Ut, re, mi, fa...' he sang. 'Well, there are different kinds of singing, aren't there? To be sure, a voice is an instrument, but an instrument may be a voice.'

The music-master stood up and walked over to a long table laid not with plates and spoons and knives and forks, as they are in the refectory, but with beautiful instruments.

I could see the instruments were arranged in families: instruments with strings, and instruments you blow, some silver, some gold, some made of dark wood with reeds in their mouths – and percussion instruments – drums and cymbals and triangles.

I gazed at them all, and my heart pounded.

'Well,' Father Antonio asked me, 'which one will you try?'

I pointed to one of the instruments with strings. Not the father or the mother: they were both taller than I am. And not the little one.

Father Antonio picked her up, and the bow lying beside her.

'Do you know her name?' he asked me.

I raised my right hand to my shoulder and swept it sideways, away from my body, to tell him that I didn't. The instrument gleamed; she shone. She was shapely.

'Viola,' he told me. 'Good choice!'

*

Father Antonio strolled over to the fire
blazing in the hearth.

Our old orphanage dog, Marco, was lying
in front of it, asleep. He's usually asleep.

The music master beckoned me.

'Warm your hands,' he told me. 'I can see
you've got a warm heart, but to play the viola,
you need warm fingers as well.'

Then he twisted the metal nut at one end of
the bow, and tightened the hair.

'Horsehair,' he told me, 'and the strings are
made of catgut.'

I opened my eyes wide.

'Oh yes!' he said, smiling. 'This viola can
miaow and neigh if you're not careful. But she's
also one of the instruments that angels play.'

Then Father Antonio tucked the viola
under his chin and cradled her with his left
arm and laid his long white fingers across her
strings. He raised the bow with his right hand
and slowly drew it across the bottom string.

'Now you try,' he told me.

*

When I drew the bow across her bottom
string, the viola didn't sing, and she didn't
miaow or neigh. She brayed like a donkey.
Father Antonio winced as if he were sucking
a lemon, but then he laughed.

'Everyone's the same,' he exclaimed. 'My
music room's a bestiary. I really must compose
something for cats and horses and donkeys
and mice and pigeons and mosquitoes and
winged lions.' The music master waved his
arms and roared. 'And all the other creatures
in Venice!'

'Compose one for larks, Father Antonio,'
Sister Cattina suggested.

'Larks,' he repeated. 'Violins, then. Just for
violins.'

'Or lobsters!' Sister Cattina said,
making her fingers into claws.

'Yes!' exclaimed Father Antonio.
'Clicking and clacking. And whistling when
you drop them into the pot.'

*

After I had drawn the bow across the C string and the G, and then the D and A strings, Father Antonio pushed out his lower lip. He walked over to the long table and picked up another instrument.

'This is a flute,' Father Antonio told me. 'A beak flute, because her mouthpiece looks like a beak! Her song is more lovely than any other instrument.'

He placed the flute between my hands.

'She makes a beautiful, breathy, birdlike song. I want you to learn to play her.'

Gently I blew, and the flute began to sing. I heard her. I heard her soft breathing.

The music master closed his eyes. He smiled.

'Yes,' he said slowly. 'Yes. I rather thought so.'

I'll never forget a word
of what Father Antonio said next:
'Some things in our lives, we
think about, we hope for, we dream of,
we half-believe. But some we just know. And
what I know, Laura, is that if you practise
and learn to play this instrument, the
day will come when angels stop and
listen to you.'
That's what he said.
My eyes grew hot with tears.

*

Father Antonio replaced the flute on the long
table and asked me and Sister Cattina to follow
him.

He led us to the far end of the music room,

and then we climbed up past
the grille, into the gallery.

The grille is so pretty. I know
it's made of iron but it looks like loosely
woven knitting. Like a cat's cradle. Or
a cobweb. 'Thirteen steps,' said the
music master.

'A little nearer to heaven,' Sister Cattina
added.

'This is where my choir and the orchestra
practise,' Father Antonio told me. 'Sixty girls
and women in all. My daughters of music.
And because they're playing behind this
grille, the audience can see only their
silhouettes. If they could see so many
beautiful girls, it would only distract them
from the music.'

'Especially the men,' added Sister
Cattina. 'You should hear some of them.
One Frenchman told me that while he was
listening, he "felt a tremor of love such as he'd
never felt before".'

When we came down the steps from the
gallery, Father Antonio told me: 'To begin
with, Laura, you may borrow the flute – but
you must be sure to look after her. When
you've finished practising, tuck her up in
her case.'

I put my right hand to the side of my head
and closed my eyes.

'Yes!' Father Antonio said, smiling. 'Tuck her
up and tell her to go to sleep. Now, then. I'll
teach you myself. Up here in this music room.'

It's a good thing I can't speak, because I wouldn't have known what to say.

'Two lessons each week,' Father Antonio said briskly. 'But you must practise each day. It's hard work learning to play any instrument, and learning to read music.'

Sister Cattina sniffed. 'You may have been chosen,' she said. 'You may be a daughter of Music, but you'll still have your daily duties and your reading and writing lessons with Sister Barbara, the same as all the other girls. Rosana, Angelica, Peta, everyone.'

'However...' said the music master, smiling at Sister Cattina.

'However!' the nun repeated. 'Seeing as Father Antonio has chosen you, we will give you this favour, this pride of place. You will have your own separate room.'

'A quiet place to practise in,' Father Antonio told me. 'And to sleep in without being disturbed. As the Holy Bible says, "a room apart, a place of peace".'

Sister Cattina narrowed her eyes. 'Where does it say that?' she demanded.

Father Antonio winked at me. 'Somewhere or other,' he replied. 'And if it doesn't, well, it should!'

Not many girls are chosen. All the others sleep in dormitories even longer than the new-girls' room. There are thirty-two beds in the dormitory for the youngest girls, and a much older girl sleeps at each end.

No one is allowed to talk after the lanterns have been blown out, and the two older girls try to keep order.

They can't, though.

Peta said I should just see what goes on, so one night I slipped into her dormitory and

hid beneath her sheet while the nuns were
saying prayers and sprinkling holy water and
bidding everyone good night.

The moment they closed the door, the girls
started to jump from bed to bed, and scamper
up and down the aisle, and giggle and chatter.

I didn't want to go back to my own little room.

When I did, it was so quiet.

*

Because you know something won't ever
happen, it doesn't stop you longing for it.

I know I'll never be able to speak or sing
with my own voice.

I don't know why.

I wish I did know.

*

It's because of Father Antonio that I've begun
to write my diary. The Diary of an Orphan. He
said that I may not be able to speak but I can
certainly write.

'So that's what you should do,' he told me.

I frowned and shook my head. What? Write what?

'Write yesterday and today and tomorrow. Write everything from the beginning.'

I didn't really understand what he meant.

'Write all you can remember. Write what happens here each day, and your thoughts and feelings. Write what you want to happen.'

*

The girls in the dormitories are quite jealous, and they play tricks on the new daughters of music.

One night, five girls holding lanterns surrounded me in my bed. I didn't know who they were but they were older than I am.

'Who can sing the highest?' one of them demanded. 'What about you, Laura?'

They all laughed at me.

'You can be the judge then, Laura,' said another girl.

Then they all sang; they sang high and higher. They squeaked, they shrieked. I blocked my ears, and they swung their lanterns.

'Now who can sing the lowest?' asked the first girl.

Down, down, down... until they were growling and coughing.

'Almost as bad as Sister Georgia,' the second girl croaked. 'You know, the one with a moustache who says she can sing lower than the lowest man.'

'What Father Antonio says,' said one girl, 'is that he's only chosen Laura because she's mute. I heard him. He says he feels sorry for her.'

That's not true, I thought. It's not.

Is it?

*

I can whistle, though. When I purse my lips.

Our old orphanage dog, Marco, is stone deaf, and so he can't hear me. But when I lived in the country, Berto and Eva's dog could hear me from halfway across the field above our hut. First he pricked his ears, then he bounded down the slope and leaped up at me.

*

Another night, a gang of boys escaped from their side of the orphanage. They raided some of our rooms while we were eating in the refectory.

They balanced a bucket full of water on top of the door to my little room, and when I pushed it open, the bucket emptied itself over me.

Worse, it splashed all over my flute because I hadn't tucked her away inside her case. And the water half-filled the case as well.

I used my second set of clothes to dry the flute and the case.

*

I remember how it rained all that night,
outside my dark window, inside my dreams.
In the corner of my little room.

Plink …

        plink …

                PLASH …

        plink …

Musical notes. They sound like a song I almost
think I almost know.
A song I've known all my life.

           *

'Disgraceful!' said the nuns when they found
out about the raid. 'Absolutely disgraceful!
The boys know very well that all the girls'
rooms and dormitories are out of bounds.'
    Each boy who took part in the raid was
locked into a room on his own for three days,

with nothing to eat but bread and nothing to drink but water.

I don't know their names but two of the gang cornered me in the refectory.

'When we find out who ratted on us, we're going to... going to...'

'...dismember her,' said the second boy very slowly.

'It was you, Laura. It was, wasn't it?'

I shook my head. I held up the palms of my hands right in front of their faces.

'You'd better find out who it was, then,' the second boy said in a threatening voice.

The first boy grinned. 'It was worth it, anyhow!'

*

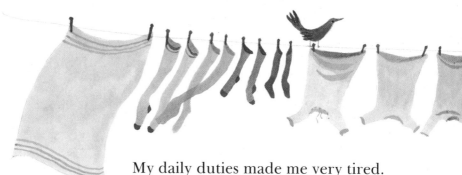

My daily duties made me very tired.
I worked down in the smelly, gloomy
kitchens with Peta, plucking chickens and
skinning rabbits, as the butcher's wife taught
me to do when I lived in the countryside. And
I had to carry out bucket after bucket of slops
and bones to the backyard.

But Peta never complains and she never
walks when she can hop or skip, and she
often laughs. Even though she can't play an
instrument or sing, she's my best friend, really.

Sister Cattina says I'm not allowed to sew
or mend, because I need to save my fingertips
for my flute.

I think it would be worse to have no hands
than no legs, because you need hands for most
kinds of work. But what about being blind?

Or deaf? Would that be
worse than being mute?
After six months, though,
the nuns changed my duty.
'New girls always begin by doing the rough
work,' Sister Cattina explained. 'Cooking
down here in the kitchens. Chopping wood
for the fires to heat the ovens and the music
room. Washing the linen. All the sweeping
and polishing.
'Yes, it's a big place, this orphanage. But
now that more girls have come
back here from the country,
Peta must start to weave.
And you, Laura, you
have to go up. Up
and up.'

I blew out my cheeks.

I didn't want to be separated from Peta.

*

I had to climb up all the stone steps to the top
of the orphanage.

Stella was waiting for me there, in the
apothecary room.

She is so beautiful. Her long hair is
different colours – copper and bronze and
gold. Her legs are long too, long as a foal's,
and she has molten chestnut eyes.

She is teaching me about plants and
medicines. Concoctions, she calls them.

When anyone in the Orphanage has a
headache or a nosebleed or a worm in one
of her teeth, or is suffering from the runs or
constipation, or keeps talking in her sleep, she
climbs up here to see us and we listen to her
and give her the right medicine.
Stella is sixteen, and her name means star.

I don't know what Laura means.

＊

'Once,' Sister Cattina told me, 'hundreds of years ago, a great poet lived here, in this very street. His name was Petrarca. Each day he wrote songs about a young woman who had captured his heart, and they were so musical, so full of love and longing, that she has never grown old.

'This young woman,' Sister Cattina said, 'her name is Laura. And apart from blessed Maria, there's no better name than that.'

＊

Father Antonio's face was as pink as his hair is red. He swung his arms and stamped his feet.

'Frozen and shuddering in the crusty snow,' he intoned, 'my teeth chattering because it's so cold, so cold…'

The music master flexed his fingers. 'I've been making a poem,' he told me. 'About this fearsome winter. Yes, shuffling along for fear

of falling over.' Father Antonio smiled. 'God willing, Laura, spring will come soon, and then I'll... I'll spring you out of here! It's time you saw a bit of Venice.'

I looked at Father Antonio, wide-eyed. I'd never seen him so high-spirited.

'*This is winter,*' he declaimed. '*Winter's stronghold. But winter brings joys unsung and untold.*'

And then he clapped his hands, and began to hum.

*

Spring came and Father Antonio kept his word.

'Come on, Laura,' he called as he saw me padding along the stone passage in my new felt shoes. 'We haven't got all morning. Well, we have, actually! Sister Cattina says you can go out until the midday meal.'

The music master appraised my newly washed shift.

'Almost like a balloon,' he said. 'And you're such a scrap of a thing. If the wind gets up, you'll fly away.'

*

Oh! This was the first time, the very first, that I'd stepped out of the orphanage front door since coming back from the countryside.

The air! I filled my lungs with clean, cool, salty tides of it.

And the spring sunlight! It tickled my nose and the lobes of my ears.

And the water-street at my feet. Curdling,

trembling, almost rippling, all the time changing from olive to violet to indigo to pewter.

But then Father Antonio touched my right shoulder with his forefinger. 'Look!' he said. 'Up there!'

A lion with wings and a huge mane was standing high over my head, on the ledge of a building. He was made of marble.

'Between his paws,' the music master told me. 'See?'

What I saw was a tortoiseshell cat. And seeing me, she stood up, yawned and arched her back, then narrowed her green eyes. She leaped down from the lion onto a lower ledge, and from there to the ground, and ran up to me.

*

The further we walked, the more beasts and
birds and fish I saw – living ones and dead
ones and stone ones.

I tugged at Father Antonio's arm, and
pointed.

A group of dogs, grinning and gossiping.

Daredevil swifts, cutting the day into white
pieces.

A cart piled with slippery heaps of fish,
gaping and silver-green and blue-gold.

A scowling monster.

A bearded man with strings of sausages tied
round his waist.

Oh! How I wished Peta could have seen
it all.

At this moment, a beautiful woman walking towards us planted herself in front of me. She narrowed her eyes, and then she spat right at my feet.

'Keep close to me,' said Father Antonio. 'Take my hand, Laura.'

I started to tremble.

'She recognised you because of your white cap,' Father Antonio told me, 'and some people in Venice, I'm sorry to say, despise children from the orphanage.'

The music master squeezed my hand.

'Yes,' he said, 'some beasts in Venice look quite like people and some people behave quite like beasts.'

Outside the cathedral, above the middle doorway, there are four rearing bronze stallions. Their eyes are dark moons. They are the rulers of the huge piazza, the city of Venice, the whole world.

Inside the cathedral, the walls and domes are covered with thousands and thousands of burnt gold pieces.

'In here,' Father Antonio whispered, 'there are so many wonders that you need a swivel-neck like a swan.'

The cathedral floor is a huge mosaic of little coloured tiles, each of them no larger than my thumbnails. They're all arranged in patterns – triangles, semi-circles, squares.

Father Antonio led me across it. He pointed.

At my feet were two birds I'd never seen before.

Birds with fierce eyes and very long necks and sapphire breasts and turquoise fantails, inlaid with saffron eyes.

'These birds are peacocks,' Father Antonio
whispered. 'They tell us that even though
each of us must one day die, not one of us will
ever die.'

I shook my head, but before Father Antonio
could explain, the cathedral organist began to
play. The scales and arpeggios of the cathedral
organ trilled through me; the great chords
thrilled me.

The music master stiffened. 'Poor man,'
he observed in a very dry voice. 'Fistfuls of
wrong notes! He has never played a right
note in his life.'

*

Sometimes I wonder whether I can hear or
see things that other people can't.

Dust dancing in a sunbeam.

A cockerel crowing so far, far away that it
seems like years ago.

But today there was something else, and
I don't quite know how to explain it.

I could sense something behind me, then
in front of me, then encircling me, and it was
invisible. A sort of lightness and brightness.

It grew strong and stronger, and it made
me want to sing and weep, weep and sing.

Then it faded, and I was alone again. As if
whatever it was had never been.

Everything was just the same as before.
The wide canal, the widest in this whole city,
smelling of salt and fish, glassy, murky green.
Longboats heaped with carrots and cabbages
and apricots and peaches. Men and women
hurrying along the stony path, talking,
laughing, calling out. And a woman, a woman
with such haunted eyes, a street singer...

Who was she? A kind of ghost. I wish I
could have asked Father Antonio.

*

'Venice may be very beautiful,' Father Antonio
said, 'but she is also very ugly. And not just
women spitting. All the pickpockets, the
gangs and feuds and backstreet fights, the
drownings.'

All the babies, I thought. Unwanted.
Abandoned.

'The backstreets can be dangerous,' Father
Antonio told me. 'That's why I always carry
my sword-stick. Keep your eyes peeled.'

The narrow passages swerve and twist.
Sometimes they were quiet as graves.
Sometimes I could hear footsteps and
voices, but couldn't tell where they were
coming from.

Three young boys ran up behind us,
waving sticks.

Father Antonio grabbed my hand but
before we reached the end of the passage,

three more boys came hurtling towards us.
They were yelling and howling.

The music master drew his sword-stick, and
slashed in front of him, behind him. The six
boys backed up against the walls.

'If I meet any of you again,' Father Antonio
threatened them, 'I'll cut you into pieces and
feed you to the pigeons.'

The passage led into a little paved square.
There was an arcade and a row of small shops
along one side.

I looked through the iron bars into their
windows. The first shop sold frilly bonnets
and silk shawls, silver beads and muffs and
cuffs, kid-gloves every colour of the rainbow,

peacocks' feathers and
much more besides.

A woman and a man were
standing in the window of the
second shop, with a little girl between
them. To begin with, I thought
they were all real. A mother and
father, and their daughter. A
family. The woman was wearing
a scarlet mask and cream cloak, and
the man was wearing a white mask
and a black cloak and a three-
cornered hat. The girl was wearing
a pair of lovely little white wings.

'This is the busiest shop
in the city during the Carnival,'
Father Antonio told me. 'It sells
the best masks in Venice.'

The third shop...

My heart began to thud.

I stared and stared. The window of the third shop was full of musical instruments. A violin with its gleaming, watery top. A shining, golden horn. A little instrument like a clarinet...

'A salmoe,' the music master said.

'...a viola, a mandolin, a cello, a bassoon...'

'Laura,' Father Antonio asked, 'do you know why we're here?'

I shook my head.

The music master splayed his long white fingers and combed back his long red hair. He gave me a lingering smile.

'To buy you a flute,' he told me. 'Of your own.'

*

As we stepped out of the shop, a bell was booming.

'Can you hear her?' Father Antonio asked me.

I was holding my flute in her case and my face was flushed. My whole body was glowing.

'The grandmother, she's called. The cathedral's noon bell. You can hear her right across the city.'

Noon! I looked up at the music master, alarmed. I pointed that it was time for us to go.

'Oh!' he exclaimed. 'You're right, yes. Sister Cattina will never forgive me.'

*

When I went up to the music room for my first lesson with my own new flute, another girl was standing beside Father Antonio.

Her shiny black hair came down to her waist. She had a white face.

'This is Silvia,' the music master told me. 'She and Susanna play the flute in the orchestra, and I've been telling her about you. How old are you, Silvia?'

'Thirteen.'

'Yes, thirteen. Now, Laura, I want Silvia to listen to you and sometimes to play with you.'

I couldn't tell what Silvia was thinking.

'We all need each other,' Father Antonio declared. 'You, Laura, to improve your skills and confidence; and you, Silvia, to listen, and learn to sing with others. As for me, I'm learning to teach, and because I teach I compose better.'

*

I wanted to show my flute to Stella more than anyone else.

I sprinted up all the stone steps, and she was already there, pounding herbs with her pestle and mortar.

I tried to catch my breath and I couldn't stop smiling. I opened my flute case, and looked up at Stella.

But all she did was push out her lower lip. She shrugged.

I moistened my lips.

Stella clicked her tongue and shook her head. 'Not now, Laura,' she told me. 'We've got better things to do.' And she reached up for one of the apothecary jars lining the shelves.

I lowered my eyes. They began to sting.

Stella swept her long fair hair away from her eyes, and clicked her tongue again. 'You can play it another time.'

*

There was a bitter argument today, and I'm not sure what it was about, though Angelica said she heard several boys flinging filthy insults about our mothers, and then they threw their spoons and platters at us, and some of us hurled them straight back. I did!

But the quarrel probably began with a squabble over food. It usually does. The boys don't get as much rice or beef stew or bread as the daughters of music, even though some of them are twice as large as we are.

Stella says she knows a boy called Danilo and he's as big as a giant and always hungry.

'He left the orphanage last year,' she told me. 'All the boys have to leave when they're sixteen and find work in the city. Danilo's training to be a stonecutter.'

The nuns were outraged when they heard about what had happened in the refectory, and we have all been punished. For the next three days, no one at all is allowed to speak in the refectory while we're breaking our fast, or during the midday meal.

'Be silent before the Lord God,' Mother
Paulina commanded us. 'The Book of
Zephaniah. Chapter one, verse seven.'

'It's all right for you, Laura,' Rosana
muttered. 'You can't speak anyhow.'

'Half the boys here are louts,' Sister Cattina
told me. 'They'll end up in prison, or get
young women pregnant. And what do you
suppose will happen to their babies?'

This morning, Silvia came to find me in my
own room, and she told me very sad news.

She said that Death had slipped in through
Susanna's barred window during the night.

I lowered my head. I covered my eyes with
my open hands.

Susanna was seventeen and she played first
flute in the orchestra. She was very, very thin
and often refused to eat.

Silvia says she will be buried under the floor of the Church of Santa Maria, where the choir and orchestra perform all their concerts, except those in our own music room.

'Once you're a daughter of music,' she observed, 'you never go away, really. Your spirit goes on singing.'

*

When I saw Father Antonio for my lesson this morning, he was very thoughtful.

'Are you practising?' he asked. 'Each day. Twice each day!'

I nodded eagerly.

'That's not what Silvia says. She tells me you talk too much!' Father Antonio smiled apologetically and coughed. 'Well, you know what I mean. No, it's not enough to have talent, Laura. You must work at your skills.'

I showed Father Antonio my puffy fingertips.

'Hmm,' he grunted.

And now another girl has
gone away. My own friend.
My Peta.
Before she pushed Peta through the
baby hatch, her mother tucked half
a token – yes, a bronze medal of Saint
Mark – into her swaddling clothes.
And in the quiet hour today, while we were
resting, her mother came back. Back here to
the orphanage.
Around her neck swung another half-medal,
and the two halves fitted exactly. I saw them.
She was wearing a sky-blue silk dress. It was
beautiful.

Peta's mother came
back for her. After eight years.

Peta sobbed.

Angelica and Julia and Anna and
Rosana and Aneta sobbed. Tears
streamed from our eyes.

We wept because Peta is wanted.
Because she's found her mother.
Because we're losing her. We wept
because we're lost.

'In life and death,' sobbed Peta, 'you're
my sisters. Now and always.'

I keep thinking something and I wish
I knew how to write it: the way that life and
death are like two halves of one circle. The way
each needs the other, and how they fit exactly.

*

When I went downstairs, and along the echoing passage to the porter's office to collect our morning package from the apothecary in the city, I could hear a woman wailing.

And then she cried out: 'No milk. None. Not one drop!'

I heard the porter asking her something.

'Away!' she cried. 'Away south, trading. Two years now.'

The porter groaned. 'So he's not the father...'

The woman gave a loud sniff, and then such a deep sigh that she sounded as if she were tired of life itself.

Slowly, I turned away and trudged back up the steep stone steps. I gave each one a name:

Stinking …
   Swaddling …
      Motherless …
         Fatherless …
            Nameless …
               Screaming …

Only when I reached the top did I remember
why I'd gone down.
   'Where's the package?' Stella demanded.
   I winced.
   'You're dumb as a doorstopper, Laura.' Stella
shook her head. 'Go on! Back down again!'
I closed my eyes.

      Motherless …
         Voiceless …
            Mindless …
               Useless …

*

Berto and Eva's hut is in the middle of a field.

During June and July it looks like a boat half-swamped in a sea of wildflowers and high waving grasses.

I wish we had flowers and grasses here, but the main courtyard is tiled, and there are only a few blades and tiny white stars in the corners of the backyard.

In high summer, we all have to wear our bonnets when we exercise in the courtyard because of the heat of the sun. The walls of the orphanage get really warm and they don't cool down again until long after sunset.

The heat is too much for poor old Marco. He collapses in the shadows, and sprawls out as if he has been shot, and sleeps all day.

Quite often it feels as if the day has got a headache, and in the evening there's a thunderstorm.

Father Antonio is writing a summer poem. He says it's all about flies and other insects, but I heard him whistling like a cuckoo, a turtle-dove, and then like a goldfinch.

'Drat!' he exclaimed. 'Clinch? Pinch? Squinch! What else rhymes with goldfinch?'

*

'You've got a good ear,' Father Antonio told me.

I signed to him that I've got two good ears, and the music master laughed. 'No, I mean you always play in tune. And you keep the beat very well.'

He smiled at me in the way he did outside the shop where we bought my flute at the beginning of spring.

'Well, Laura,' he said. 'Poor Susanna has left us. Much too soon she has left us. And when someone leaves, we are all weakened, and yet it brings us all together.'

He sighed and looked at the ground.

'For love is strong as death,' he went on. 'Isn't that what the Song of Songs reminds us? Well, I only hope that this isn't much too soon as well.'

I didn't know what he meant.

Father Antonio inspected me.

'Such a scrap of a thing,' he said. 'There's no need to look so fearful.'

I was, though.

'Now, then! An orchestra without two flutes is like… I don't know, like a woman with only half a heart. You'll have to sit out the bits that are just too difficult.'

Half-grave, half-smiling, the music master gazed at me.

'Laura,' he said, 'I'm inviting you to play in my orchestra.'

*

When Silvia led me into the music room, the whole orchestra and choir were already up in the gallery. They were talking and laughing, and playing scales and little bits and pieces.

It was the most exciting sound I've ever heard. And however often I may hear it, I think it always will be.

My heart was still thumping when the music master strode in. He smiled at Silvia and me, and bounded up the thirteen steps past the pretty grille and into the gallery. We all followed him.

Silvia led me straight to our music desk and even before we'd sat down, the music master rapped his own stand with his white baton.

He rapped it again.

'That's better,' he said, and he pointed his baton at me. 'As you see, we have a new player. Laura. Will you please welcome her?'

All around me, members of the orchestra began to tap their instruments. The string players used the backs of their bows, and the wind and brass players tapped with their knuckles. The choir began to clap.

I lowered my head. I couldn't breathe steadily.

'Laura is nine,' Father Antonio said, 'and so she's the youngest member of our orchestra. As some of you know, she is mute. But how she makes her flute sing! Please greet her after rehearsal.'

The music master adjusted the pages on his desk.

'Laura,' he called out. 'Will you give us an E?'

My lips were dry. I moistened them. I blew.

The music master pulled a little pitch-pipe out of his breast pocket, and blew it.

'Absolutely!' he announced. 'Another E please, Laura.'

The string players adjusted their willow pegs. They played chords.

All around me, the instruments of the orchestra growled and cleared their throats and fluttered and cheeped. Their players composed themselves.

Ready!

*

It was all over so quickly. That's what happens when you're really concentrating. Time stands still. Time flies!

We were rehearsing a cantata by Arcangelo Corelli for the first concert of the autumn season, and I was able to play in tune and keep the beat because I'd already been practising it. We played it right through three times, and each time Father Antonio kept stopping us, and correcting us, and encouraging us.

There are as many women as girls in the orchestra, and some are old enough to be my grandmother or even my great grandmother. They've all lived here since they were born.

Sister Georgia, the one with the moustache and the deepest voice, is the oldest. She's sixty-seven.

Everyone milled around me in the music room, and some of the women embraced me. One of them kissed both my burning cheeks.

On Sunday evening, I'm going to play in my
first concert.

That's only three days from now.

*

Playing in an orchestra is completely different
to playing on my own.

Sometimes I played, sometimes listened;
instead of waiting my turn, I sometimes
interrupted another player, sometimes I

argued, sometimes agreed.

My flute is my mouthpiece and I felt as if I was actually joining in a conversation.

*

All afternoon, Stella was friendly, and I could tell she was excited about something.

When I'd finished my duties, she said, 'That room looking over the back courtyard... the one where they keep all the spare bedding...'

I nodded.

'As soon as the nuns have blessed you and bidden you good night, get dressed and meet me there. I've got a surprise for you.'

Stella's eyes were sparkling. She put her left forefinger to her lips, and gave me a naughty smile.

*

In the half-light I crept down to the room.
Stella had already tied the corners of two
sheets together and was knotting a third to
the first two.

'We'll need four,' she said in a husky voice.

I helped, and Stella tied the last sheet to a
window bar with a double knot, and then she
slipped through the bars.

'Follow me,' she said. 'Slide down the
sheets. You'll have to jump at the bottom.'

I didn't want Stella to see I was scared.
I clamped my teeth and slid down the sheets
from knot to knot. We scooted across the
yard and unbolted the door used by all the
boatmen who deliver food to the orphanage
and collect the refuse.

I could hear rats squeaking and scampering
around the rubbish heaps, but it was almost
too dark to be sure I could see them.

*

On our way down the path leading to the great canal, four skulking figures jumped out at us and surrounded us – a clown, a brown bear, a beautiful woman with sharp black teeth, and a unicorn. Stella squeezed my right hand.

The figures danced around us and leaped at Stella and made her shriek. I thought they wanted to grab her little silver purse or something, but all they did was shriek like Stella, leap and shriek. Then they ran off, laughing.

'Horrible!' exclaimed Stella, and she shuddered.

I wished I could tell her about the shop that sells masks – that one in the arcade, next to the shop where Father Antonio bought me my own flute.

The path widened. The Grand Canal. She opened her dark arms to us.

Oh! It looked as if the August stars had fallen out of the sky into the water. Thirty of them. Forty. Even more, maybe.

They were pearly and milk-blue, but the stars nearest to us were pink as peaches – lanterns swinging in the bows of little boats.

Across the water, I could hear snatches of song, someone playing a mandolin, shouts of laughter.

'Tell me I can trust you,' Stella said.

I nodded.

'Yes, I know,' she said, and she put an arm around my shoulder.

'Danilo,' Stella murmured. 'We're meeting him. He knows how to get a boat. You can be our lookout.'

*

By the light of the lanterns, I could see Stella's liquid eyes looked almost twice as large as they usually do.

'It's called belladonna,' she told me later. 'I put a drop in each eye. It makes your pupils larger.'

Stella was right. Danilo is huge. You can see the muscles in his forearms and neck.

'Now, Laura,' he instructed me, 'you hold the lantern and keep watch. Just signal if any boat comes close and I'll paddle us away from her. Understand?'

I nodded.

'We'll sit here and talk, and things,' Stella said, and she giggled. She wagged her left forefinger. 'No turning round, Laura.'

'I'll drop you overboard,' Danilo warned me.

*

The lantern cast a soft pool of light over the water in front of us. My thoughts drifted.

After a while, I completely forgot about Stella and Danilo.

Everything, I thought, everything keeps changing. Changing shape, changing colour, changing sound. That's how it is in Venice.

So then I changed the water around me, the water and our little bobbing boat. I changed them into words, and words into music:

Soft hollow, ribs and ridge,
Sway and jig, jolt then surge,
Slip and slop, draw back, meet,
Sing in tune, and follow
the beat ...

Just before dawn, a chilly white sea-mist
unscrolled itself over the lagoon and the city.
She blurred edges; she dampened sounds.
And she cocooned the moon and the planets
and stars.

By the time Stella and I got back to the
orphanage, I was shivering. I was anxious
in case Father Antonio saw how tired I was
during my lesson with him, and even more
anxious that we might be caught.

If we are, I thought, I won't be allowed to
play in the concert. My first concert. And his
first concert of the autumn season. I'll fail
Father Antonio.

When Stella quietly opened the door into
the courtyard, I saw at once that the ghostly
sheet-rope wasn't there. It had gone.

I clutched Stella's arm. I was terrified.
Stella didn't seem alarmed, though. She
glanced up at the window of the bedding
room and then cupped her hands to her
mouth. Three times she hooted like a

hunting barn owl.

Almost at once, the sheet-rope was pushed out between the bars, and lowered above our heads.

Stella smiled at me. 'Signorina,' she said in her husky voice, 'I really don't know what you've been doing, up half the night!' She embraced me. 'Go on now. Reach and grab each knot as soon as you can. I'll give you a leg up.'

*

Sister Cattina helped me to put on the dress that I'm to wear whenever I play in a concert in the Church of Santa Maria or in our music room. It's made of white muslin, loose and puffy and completely shapeless.

Stella would just laugh at it.

'Cool and comfortable to play in,' Sister Cattina told me.

In the church, we play behind an iron grille, just as we do in our own music room, so the audience cannot quite see us but can see only our silhouettes.

Once we had processed into the church, and settled at our music desks, the audience surged in below us and every seat was taken.

Our desks were lit with candles, and so were all the window ledges in the church.

The orchestra began to tune up around me. A shiver ran up and down my spine, down and up, and then it spread out across my shoulders.

'Laura,' Father Antonio called out. 'Please give us an E.'

First, we performed the piece I'd rehearsed with everyone. I was able to play in tune and follow the beat, and at the end the audience clapped.

After this, the choir and orchestra played a new concerto by Father Antonio, one that I haven't practised or rehearsed, so I sat and listened. There were parts for five solo instruments, and the music master explained to our audience that this was so that not one but five girls would each have the chance to shine.

Silvia was one of them! She played on her own.

When she had finished, I stroked her left arm, but she only gave me a frightened look.

The audience clapped again. They cheered. So Father Antonio asked the orchestra to play the whole concerto for a second time.

When we processed out of the church after the audience had all gone, it was just beginning to rain.

I still felt excited. For a long time I've been sitting up, listening to the rain, writing this.

*

Plink …

plink …

PLASH …

plink …

In the watches of the night.
Like a cradle, rocking.
Sometimes I think I hear you.
Do you love music too?

The drops of water falling onto my stone floor are minims and crotchets, quavers and semi-quavers.
Like a song I almost think I almost know.
Like a song you sang to me.

Even though we weren't caught, I think the nuns suspect us.

Sister Cattina says that, instead of working any more with Stella, I'm to have a new daily duty. She says Father Antonio wants me to dust all our music desks and polish his stand in the gallery of the music room, and to fit all the new candles.

I know Stella was using me when she took me to meet Danilo, but I do still like her. I like learning about medicines, and I wish I could still work with her.

I made a sour face and stuck out my tongue, and Sister Cattina saw me.

*

When I went up to the music room for my flute lesson, Silvia was waiting for me.

'Father Antonio isn't well,' she told me. 'He wants you to go to his composing room.'

The music master was sitting at a table

under the window. He was snuffling and
wheezing.

'Laura,' he growled.

He dashed down a few more notes on his
manuscript paper.

I watched him and pretended to compose
notes in mid-air.

Father Antonio sniffed. 'I compose fast,'
he croaked. 'Faster than any copyist. But not
when I'm feeling like this.'

He wheezed again. 'This tightness in my
chest, it'll be the death of me. I can't teach you
today, Laura. You must practise instead. I'm
getting worse and worse but you need to get
better and better.'

When I opened the door, three little girls
had their ears pressed against it.

At once they ran away, squealing and
singing out: 'Laura, Laura, Antonio adores
her! Laura, Laura...'

*

Plink ...

plink ...

PLASH ...

plink ...

For a long while I listened.

I heard you. I heard you sing my heart. The song you sang to me.

I picked up my flute, and moistened my lips...

Later, I slept.

＊

I took my Heartsong to my lesson.

'Ah!' said Father Antonio. 'I'm feeling better but now you're looking worse. Pink cheeks, pink eyes. What's wrong?'

Nervously, I gazed up at him.

He understood.

I played my song.

Father Antonio gave me a searching, gentle look. 'Where did you hear this?' he asked me.

I shook my head, then I covered my heart with my right hand.

'Will you play it again?'

Father Antonio closed his eyes. His eyelids trembled.

'Laura,' he said. 'It's very lovely. Like a lullaby. Rocking. It's tender yet forlorn. Da capo!'

I frowned.

'Play it again. One more time.'

Again the music master closed his eyes.

'Yes,' he murmured. 'Somehow it's new yet old. Like a memory. Shall I note it down for you?'

Father Antonio picked up
his quill and dipped it into his inkwell.
He paused, and then his fingers danced
over the manuscript paper.

I watched him note down my song.

*

In front of Berto and Eva's hut, there is a
rickety old pergola covered with pink roses
and twined with creeper. When the roses fade
and droop, the green creeper
turns the colour of onion skins and
scarlet and carmine.

In summer the sun was so hot it
blistered my skin, but in autumn the
storm-flies buzzed, clouds tore
themselves into pieces, the west

wind blustered and pine trees shooshed.

In the countryside, no two days were the same. I could see the year growing older.

But here in the orphanage, all our days and even our birthdays are very much alike. We wake, we eat, we do our duties, we go to our reading and writing and music lessons and if we're daughters of music, we rehearse.

When we exercise in the courtyard, the day is either hot or humid or chilly or freezing, and the sky is a white or grey or blue flag stretched over our heads. That's just about all we know of Venice, and the four seasons.

The nuns aren't sure exactly when each of us was born, and so they say our birthdays are on the day we were delivered here. The day we were pushed through the hatch.

So I know that at least six months of my life have been lost.

How old was I before I was born here? The world is growing older, and I'm older than I am.

The whole orchestra was sitting up in the gallery, making ready, and while Father Antonio riffled through his score, Silvia and I practised a few bars together. Then she broke off, and screwed up her eyes.

'Wrong!' she wailed. 'Again.'

I frowned and shook my head.

'No!' she exclaimed. 'Me! I'll never be any good. Not like you.'

I grabbed Silvia's left arm and dropped my head onto her shoulder. If only I could have told her how good she is. If only I could have reminded her that Father Antonio wrote a concerto especially for her and four other soloists.

'No,' declared Silvia. 'As if it's not bad enough to be locked away in this orphanage, with nothing, nothing!' Then she burst into tears.

I felt so sad for her. Silvia's much, much

better than I am, but I can feel she's jealous of me.

The music master rapped his stand, and everyone grew quiet.

'Before we rehearse,' he began, 'let me remind you that Laura has now played with us for six months. She has served her apprenticeship.'

Everyone tapped their instruments with the backs of their bows or their knuckles, and the choir clapped, just as they did when I came to my first rehearsal.

Father Antonio smiled at me. 'So here's an early birthday present for you. From today, everyone will call you "Laura the Flute".'

My heart somersaulted. I turned at once to Silvia and tried to hug her, but I felt her stiffen.

Even so, I still think we can be true friends.

*

While I was practising, there was a tap at my door. Stella put her head round it.

'Laura?' she asked, with a gay smile. 'Laura the Flute?'

I was happy to see her.

'The nuns have found me work with an apothecary in the city,' she told me, 'and his family will give me lodging. He's trying me out for three months, and after that he'll pay me.'

Stella is so… exuberant. Is that a word? She filled my little room with her own high spirits.

I made myself as tall as I could, then I puffed out my chest, and flexed my arm muscles.

Stella laughed. 'Danilo!' she exclaimed. 'Yes, I'll be able to see him as often as I want to. He likes you, Laura. When the time comes, we're going to call our first daughter by your name. I'm starting tomorrow!'

My eyes grew hot with tears.

'I'll come back and see you,' Stella said.

'I promise you, Laura.'

That's what Peta promised, I thought. But she hasn't come back. My best friend. She promised me and Angelica and Julia and Anna and Rosana and Aneta, and said we were her sisters. But once girls go away, they never come back.

Stella embraced me. 'Whenever you...' she began. Then she paused. 'Laura,' she whispered, 'think of me. And I'll remember you.'

She turned and ran out of the room.

*

I could hear raised voices.

'No! No, Antonio!'

'Yes!'

'Can't it wait?'

I recognised Sister Cattina's voice, and only she would speak to the music master like that. The greatest composer there has ever been.

'No,' said Father Antonio. 'I've already told you.'

'Why not tomorrow? It's almost sundown already and so cold that hell itself is freezing over. You're so stubborn!'

Carrying my flute in her case, and ready for my lesson, I waited just outside the music room.

Sister Cattina whistled like a bubbling kettle. 'Well, I don't know.'

'You're an angel!' Father Antonio exclaimed, and he clapped his hands.

'Wrap up warm, and make quite sure Laura does as well. And no standing around. You know how frail you are.'

'A frail child of dust,' Father Antonio chanted, 'with a guardian angel.'

'And we can't do with losing you,' added Sister Cattina. 'Or losing Laura, for that matter.'

The music master laughed. 'Who was lost is found again,' he sang out. 'Saint Luke, chapter thirteen.'

'You and your biblical verses,' said Sister Cattina, and she clicked her tongue. 'Now be sure to bring Laura back in good time... Are you listening?'

'I certainly am,' said Father Antonio. 'Back to the refectory in good time for her bread and wine.'

*

Sister Cattina was right. It was only early November, but the wind was blowing in from the sea, and the bitter cold was freezing the veins and arteries of Venice. I could hear the windows of the grand houses alongside the orphanage shuddering in their frames.

'I've known worse,' Father Antonio said. 'Cold so crackling a man could snap his moustache.'

I gasped.

'I saw your shadow,' he went on. 'I knew you were listening outside the music room.'

I gave him a guilty look.

'So where are we going this time?' the music master asked. 'And why was I so insistent?' Then he began to whistle a cheerful jig. 'Yes, where are we going?'

There was almost no one about. Just a few people scurrying along the arcades of the huge square in front of the cathedral, and a white dog with black spots, and a black dog with white spots, and two lovers in each other's arms, innocent of the weather, wrapped up in one another.

As we crossed a steep little bridge, I could see that the water in the narrow canal had already curdled. The two carved swans standing on the keystones of the bridge looked down their beaks at it.

'I come this way quite often,' Father Antonio told me, 'to play chamber music in the house of some friends. You've brought your flute, haven't you?'

I looked at him anxiously.

He can't really want me to play before his friends, I thought. Or even to play with them? Surely he can't.

'Quite often, yes,' the music master repeated, 'and I bring my ears with me.'

My ears – they both felt numb!

'Stop!' said Father Antonio in a low voice. He squeezed my right arm. 'Listen!'

*

I held my breath.

Not far in front of us, the arms of another bridge climbed and clasped each other across a much wider, much darker canal.

At each end of the bridge, there was an iron stand and a flickering lantern.

Little snowflakes were just beginning to dizzy around and feather us.

I saw there was someone leaning against the far side of the bridge.

I clutched Father Antonio's arm, and he raised his forefinger to his lips.

Time passed, I don't know how long.

Whoever it was began to sing...

Her song – I recognised it.

At once I recognised it.

Her voice was quite foggy. But around her shoulders there grew a sort of lightness and brightness. It encircled her.

My own Heartsong. I felt so stricken. I felt sick and scared.

Has Father Antonio taught her to sing it? Why? Because he said it was so lovely, and he wants everyone in the city to share it? Or... or...

I realised I was trembling.

*

'Take your flute out of her case,' the music master instructed me.

My fingers were so cold I kept fumbling.

'Now moisten your lips.'

My heart was hammering.

'Be calm, Laura,' Father Antonio murmured. 'All will be well.'

My breath was jerky.

'Each day of her life,' he told me, 'since that dreadful day she had to leave you at the orphanage, she has ached for you just as you have ached for her. She kept you for as long as she possibly could,' said the music master, 'as long as she could – and even longer. She says you were the most beautiful girl in the world. And she's never forgotten, not one quaver or semi-quaver of who you are.'

A great lump moved up and down inside my throat.

'Now play, Laura. Laura the Flute.'

I played for my life. I played as if for the first time.

The song you left with me. The song you took away. The song I've kept in my heart.

Plink ...

plink ...

PLASH ...

plink ...

My shining tears dripped onto my flute.

The music master laid his right hand on my shoulder.

He stooped, and kissed my tear-stained cheeks.

*

I climbed the stone steps. I skeltered across the bridge.

My black cloak flapped and, in the owl-light, I could hear all the birds and beasts in Venice – the herring-gulls and cormorants and cockerels, even the crocodiles and high horses and the winged lions – all of them beginning to tune up.

My cloak flapped and I skeltered across the bridge.

I reached out and she reached out.

'Laura,' she breathed.

Mama!

FROM THE AUTHOR

When you entered this book, you stepped into the Ospedale della Pietà (the nearest translation is 'hospice'). It was an orphanage and music school run by nuns, and there were three other institutions like this in early 18th-century Venice, caring for people who were war-wounded or homeless, people suffering from incurable diseases, and beggars.

The young, redheaded man, the director of music: he was Antonio Vivaldi. He was born just a couple of hundred metres away, and was already known as one of the greatest composers in Europe.

Around the Ospedale, there was plenty of noise – after all, there were no fewer than 800 children here. About sixty of them were boys, and they had to leave and find jobs in the city after their sixteenth birthdays.

Plenty of noise, not least in the kitchens, but also the sound of music everywhere, being practised, being performed. But these sounds all came from inside this rather chilly building. With its thick stone walls, it was completely cut off from the hubbub and the colour and the shouting and splashing of the city.

Around the shoulders of the Ospedale the sun shone, rain fell and so the seasons turned. The director of music was alive to all this. He lived between worlds. And in one of his greatest and most-loved works, 'The Four Seasons', he brilliantly portrayed the times and tides of the year.

Vivaldi wrote many pieces for the sixty girls in his choir and orchestra, and a number of his sonatas and concerti were not for one but a group of instruments (molti strumenti) so that several girls could each have a solo part and a starring role. They played so sweetly that a king and a pope and many great people travelled across Europe to hear them. Ah, but not to see them! The girls played in a gallery behind an iron grille, and all you could see were little glimpses.

The girls in this book may seem quite tough, some of them. But of course they often wondered about who their mothers (and fathers) were and whether they'd ever come back for them. Sometimes they were lonely. They ached. They made intense friendships. They laughed; they argued; they were jealous. Some were confident creatures; some not. Some were as fit as fiddles; some far from well.

And one girl, she was aged nine and mute. She couldn't speak but she could play the flute. How she could play. And her music filled her with longings and half-memories. This girl's name was Laura, and Jane Ray found her hiding in the Ospedale library – just a name, an entry in a list of all the girls admitted here. And now, together, we have rediscovered her and listened to her: Laura and her heartsong.

K.C-H

FROM THE ILLUSTRATOR

On my first magical trip to Venice, in the Vivaldi
Museum, I found a great leather bound ledger,
displayed under glass, listing the names of all the
foundling babies left at the Ospedale della Pieta.
Anna
Christiana
Elena
Eva
Katerina
Klaudia
On and on they go, name after name, life after
little life, scrawled in a spidery hand.

I stood transfixed – all these children, all these
stories.

Music drifted through the open window, from

a rehearsal in the church next door, pigeons called, voices drifted up from the canal below.

Lavinia

Libera

Luigia

Lucia

I came to the bottom of the page:

Laura... no. 3170, born 1724

Next to the open page with Laura's name, were tokens left by the tragic mothers – a bead, a cross, a scrap of ribbon, a tiny baby vest: rough linen, with a scarlet thread at the neck that pulled at my heart.

My head swam with pictures and a story, or elements of a story: a beautiful city filled with sound and movement – lapping water, music, raucous street cries, bells and birds, and winged lions.

The soft greys and greens of the water, the shadows and reflections, the colour of ancient stone.

A child, silent, alone, motherless.

And flowing through it, like the dark canal waters, a song...

I filled a sketchbook with pictures and notes.

I tried to pull the threads and fragments of the story together.

But somehow, it eluded me.

I could see the story – the pictures were alive and bright in my imagination. I knew who Laura was, knew what she looked like.

But the story itself, Laura's story, kept slipping from my grasp like a dream on waking.

I talked to Kevin Crossley-Holland. He knew exactly what to do. He took the scraps and fragments, discarded some, created many others, and built them all into a wonderful, solid home for Laura, the beautiful story that you have just read.

J.R